Miss Lee and the Mosquito

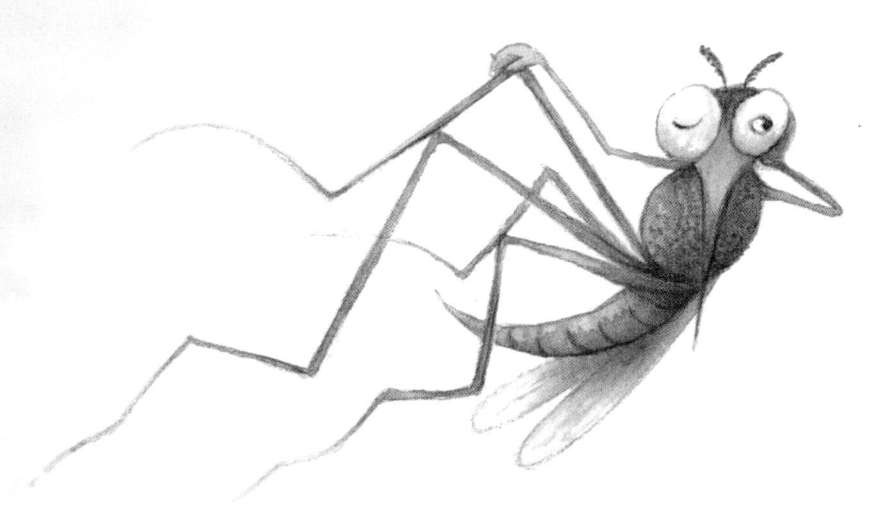

Maria L Denjongpa

Illustrated by Anna Vojtech

SCHOLASTIC
New York Toronto London Auckland
Sydney New Delhi Hong Kong

Foreword

In most parts of the world, people slap mosquitoes (and anything else they find irritating) without a second thought. In Sikkim, little kids are taught to refrain from killing.

Just as travelling expands one's understanding of the world, reading about different cultures at an early age opens kids' minds and prepares them for a life of empathy and creativity.

This book encourages kids to ask big questions—about patience, trying to keep your friend's word and not killing when you feel like it. It is a book to foster discussions and open the minds of young and old, alike.

Maria L Denjongpa

When Miss Lee went to visit Sikkim,
she slept in her friend's shrine room.

She loved the statues of Buddha. She loved the candlelight. She loved the sweet smell of incense and the silver offering bowls.

But she did NOT love the mosquito that buzzed around her ear at night. Every evening at nine o'clock she'd lay her beautiful black hair on the pretty pink pillow, and a big mosquito would fly next to her ear and make a most irritating sound.

Miss Lee wanted to kill it. WHAP! But just when she reached over to turn on the light, she remembered her friend had said it wasn't good to kill anything in the shrine room. Not even a tiny bug.

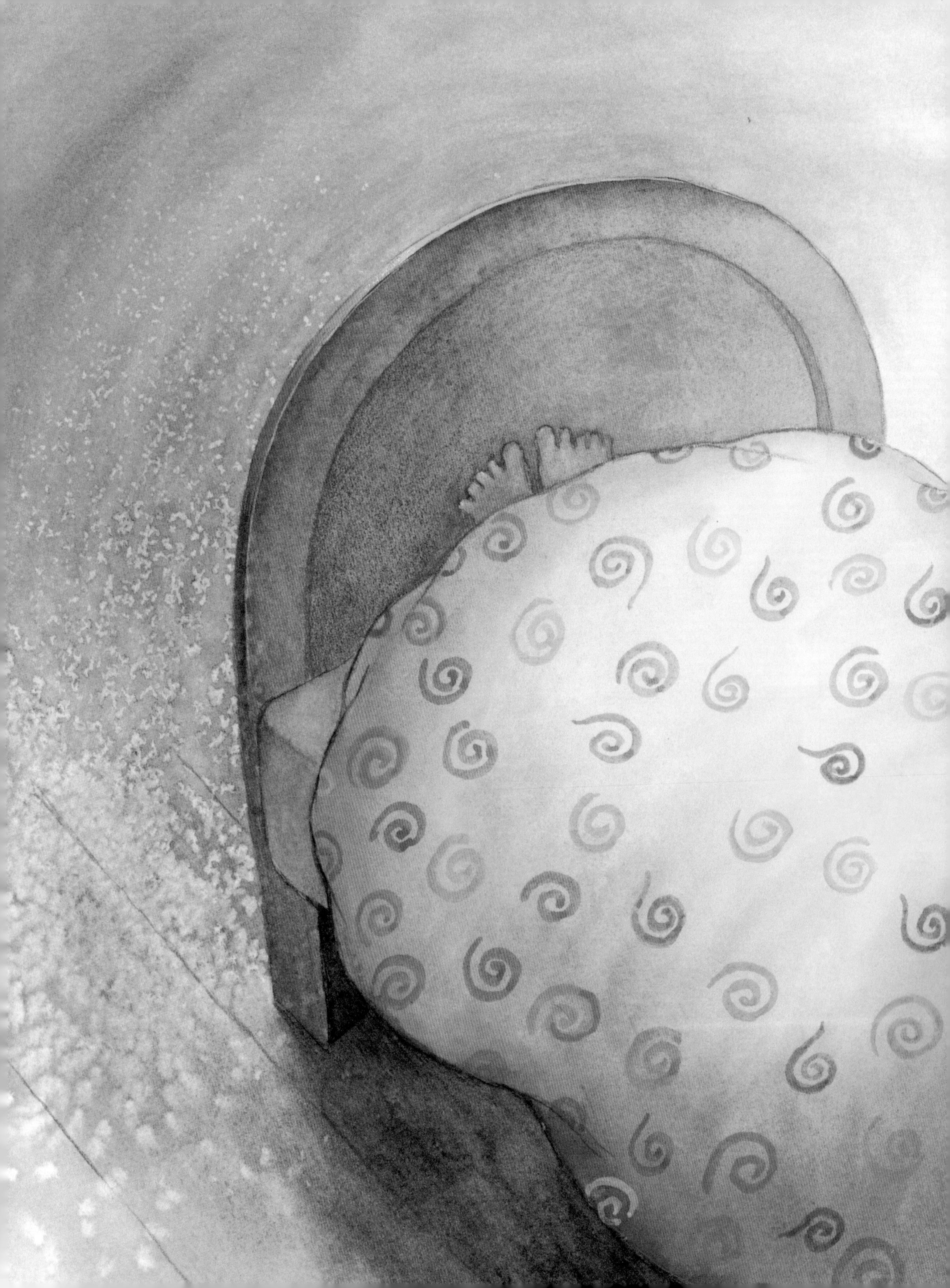

So Miss Lee rolled back onto the middle of the bed. She looked up into the dark. Everything was quiet. The buzzing mosquito was gone. She thought how happy her friend would be that she had not killed it. Miss Lee felt happy, too. Until ...

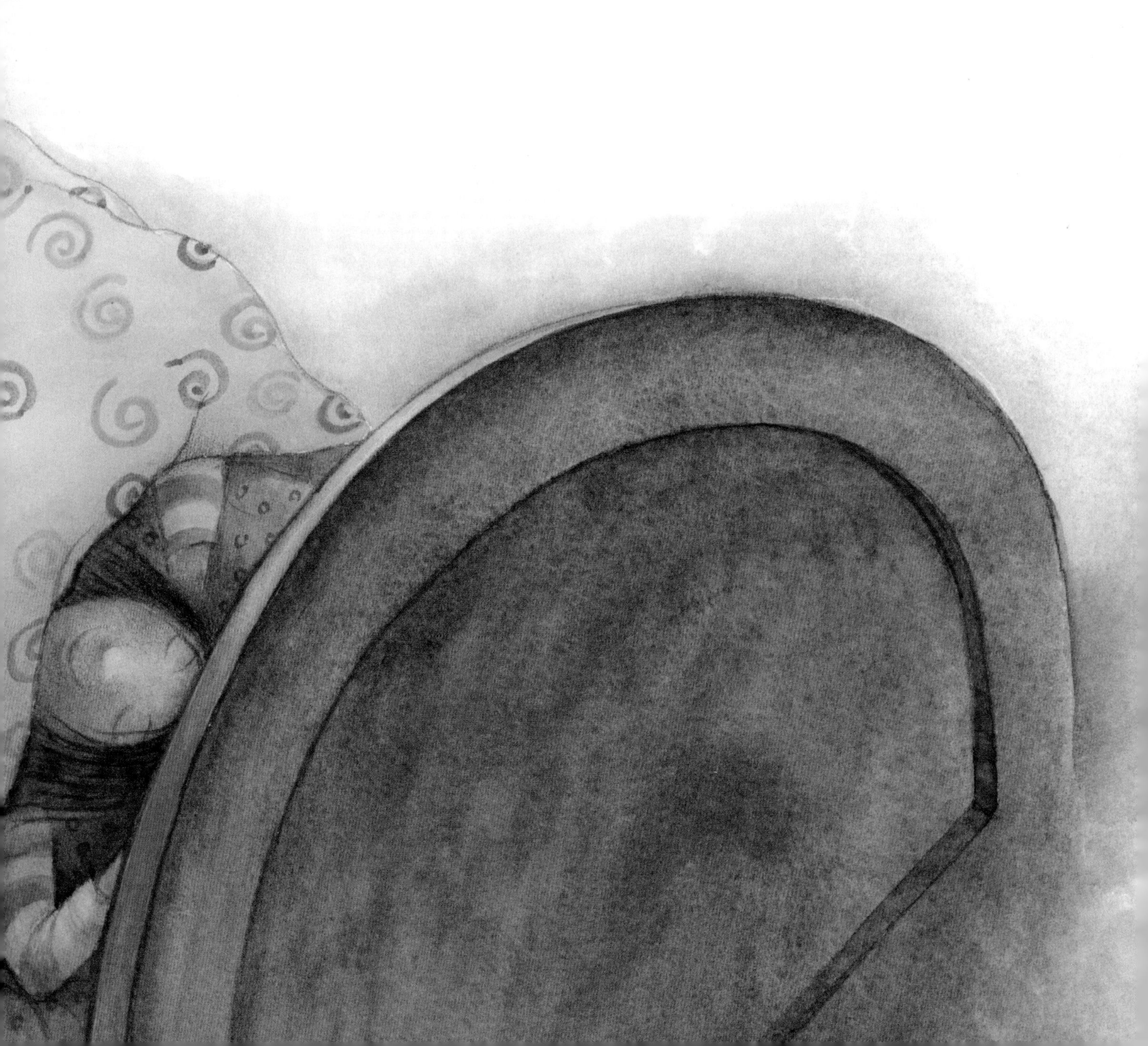

zzzZZZZZzzzzzz ...
zzzZZZZzzzzzzz ...
zzzZZZZZZzzzzzz ...
zzzzZZZZZZzz ...

Miss Lee pulled the blankets over her head.

But the buzzing didn't go away.

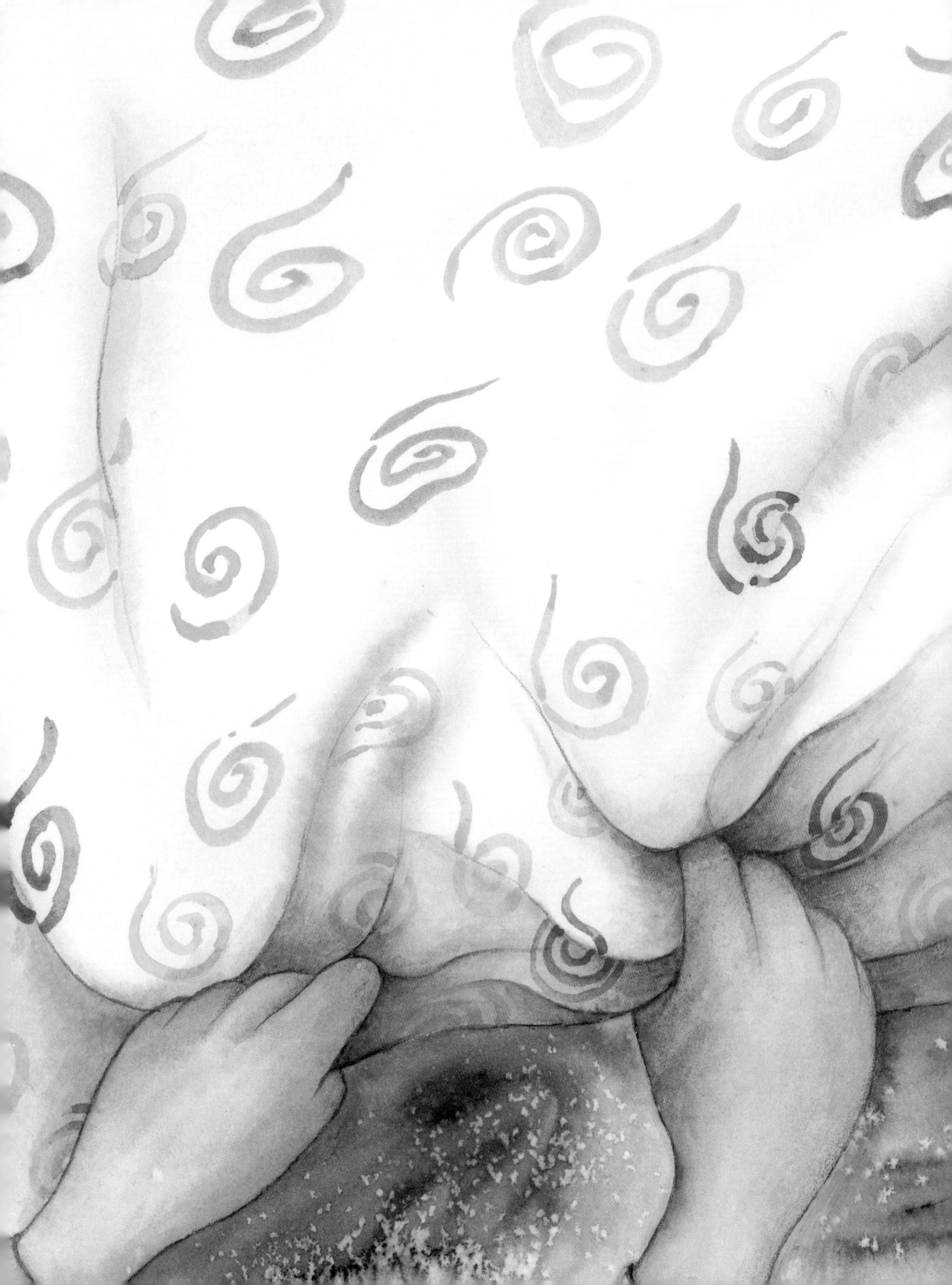

She shook the blanket as hard as she could.

But the buzzing didn't go away.

She waved her hands in big circles around her head.

But the buzzing didn't go away.

She blew big puffs of air in every direction.

But the buzzing didn't go away.

She clapped her hands and shouted, 'I can't take it anymore!'

But the buzzing didn't go away.

She sat up straight and prayed to the Buddhas on the shrine.

But the buzzing didn't go away.

Finally, Miss Lee got out of bed and walked into the living room with the blanket and the pillow piled up in her arms. She stretched out on the couch next to the window and closed her eyes.

She heard a Tata growling up the mountain and a dog howling in the village below. She heard a man singing a slow, sad song and a woman shouting, 'Who's that?'

But she did not hear the mosquito.
Not a single buzz.
Miss Lee waited.

But the only sound was the cow across the street letting out a loud, low MOOO.

Miss Lee turned towards the window and fell into a deep, delicious sleep.

Until ...